THE PUPPY PLACE

SCHOLASTIC INC.
New York Toronto London Auckland
Sydney Mexico City New Delhi Hong Kong

For Caroline, the original Bean

ISBN 978-0-545-08350-8

Cover art by Tim O'Brien
Original cover design by Steve Scott

22 21 20 18 19/0

Printed in the U.S.A. 40

First printing, October 2008

CHAPTER ONE

"How about Dorothy and the Scarecrow?" Lizzie asked.

"Hmmm . . ." Maria considered the idea.

"It would be great!" Lizzie's eyes lit up. "Buddy could be Toto. I could carry him in a picnic basket, just like Dorothy does in *The Wizard of Oz.*"

Lizzie Peterson loved Halloween. It was fun to dream up great costumes — even though she usually ended up being something simple, like a gypsy or a hobo. It was fun to be out in the streets of Littleton after dark on a fall evening — even though it was usually so cold or rainy that Mom made her wear a jacket over her costume. And, of course, it was fun to watch her trick-or-treat bag fill up little by little until it was bulging with candy — even though Lizzie and her brothers were only allowed to eat two pieces a day. By Thanksgiving, whatever was left was stale and hardly worth unwrapping and chewing.

Halloween this year would be even more fun than usual, for two reasons. First of all, Lizzie and her best friend, Maria, (and Charles and the Bean, Lizzie's younger brothers) had been invited to ride on Chief Olson's fire truck in the Littleton Halloween parade. Lizzie knew Chief Olson because her dad was a firefighter, too. But the truck that they'd be riding on wasn't one of the town's regular fire trucks. No, this was a really cool antique fire truck that belonged to Chief Olson. He kept it inside a giant garage behind his house. Lizzie could not wait to see how jealous everybody would be when they watched her drive by on the gleaming red truck, with its shiny brass fittings. That's why she just *had* to come up with an especially good costume this year.

The other reason Halloween would be special

was because this year Buddy would be part of it. Buddy was the Petersons' little brown puppy, and Lizzie loved him more than anything.

The Peterson family had fostered lots of puppies who needed homes — taking care of them until they found the perfect forever family for each one — but although Buddy had started out as a foster puppy, he had ended up as a permanent member of the family. Which still felt so, so amazing to Lizzie. She and Charles and the Bean (whose real name was Adam) had wanted a dog of their own for so long, and now they had one! Not only that, they had *Buddy*, the best dog *ever*.

"I love you, Buddy," Lizzie whispered right then, into her puppy's silky ear. He was curled up all warm and sleepy on her lap at that very moment, while she and her best friend sat at the kitchen table after school eating apples and string cheese and planning their costumes.

Maria was still thinking about Lizzie's idea. She reached over and patted Buddy's soft fur.

"Why do *you* get to be Dorothy?" she asked. "What if I want to be Dorothy?"

Lizzie thought for a moment. Maybe *The Wizard of Oz* theme wasn't the best plan after all. "Okay, how about this? We could be fairies. Buddy could be an elf or a toadstool or something."

"Maybe," Maria said. "But I thought you said fairies were stupid costumes."

"What?" Lizzie looked confused.

"During lunch today, at school. Remember? We were all talking about costumes, and you said how sick you were of everybody being fairies, and how fairy costumes were totally *over*."

"Oh. Right." Lizzie sort of remembered.

Maria frowned at her. "You don't even remember? You were spouting off opinions all over the place. Not that anybody even *asked* your opinion. In fact, Shanna Garbeck told me afterward that she felt like an idiot because she had been planning on being a fairy."

Oops. "Oh, well." Lizzie shrugged and stuck her

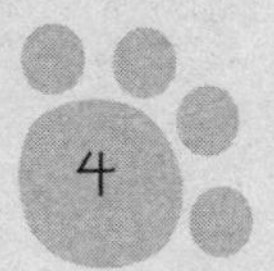

nose into the soft, sweet-smelling fur on Buddy's neck. She kissed him five times in a row. Buddy was so lovable!

"You know . . ." Maria said. She looked down at the table and spoke very carefully. "Sometimes I'm almost a little embarrassed when you do that. I mean, it's cool that you have strong opinions, but maybe it would be nice if you could wait until you're *asked* for your opinion, instead of just offering it like that."

Lizzie stared at Maria. "You're *embarrassed*?" she asked. "Why?"

"Because I'm your best friend, I guess." Maria frowned and waved her hand as if trying to get rid of a bad smell in the air. "Look, forget it. Let's go back to talking about costumes."

Lizzie did go back to talking about costumes. But she did not "forget it." She couldn't. This was not the first time that somebody had told Lizzie that she was too outspoken. Her mom had said so more than once, and even her dad had mentioned it, laughingly. "That's our Lizzie!" he'd said. "Always has an opinion — and she's always ready to share it!"

As she and Maria talked, Lizzie felt hot all over, even though it was cool in the kitchen. Silently, she vowed yet again to work harder at keeping her opinions to herself, at least until somebody *begged* for her thoughts.

"Hey!" Charles came into the kitchen, slamming the door behind him. "Wait'll you hear *this* one!"

Maria and Lizzie both groaned. Lately, Charles and his best friend, Sammy, had been driving everybody *crazy* — in a new way. It was bad enough when they were going through their knock-knock joke phase. But now they had decided to write a book: *101 Dog Jokes*, it was going to be called. Lizzie figured she had already heard about *five* hundred and one.

"Okay, ready?" Charles asked. He was already giggling. "What kind of dog does Dracula have?"

He finally managed to squeak out the question. Charles was always his own best audience.

"I give up," Lizzie said.

"Me, too," Maria agreed.

"A bloodhound!" Charles crowed. He cracked up, barely seeming to notice that the two girls were groaning, not laughing. "That's definitely one for the book!" Still laughing, he went to the fridge to look for a snack.

"Where's Sammy?" Lizzie asked.

"Home," Charles mumbled, around a mouthful of grapes. "Working on his poster for Fire Prevention Week. He really wants to win the contest this year."

Lizzie and Maria had already made their posters, even though they both knew that Noah Burke would win the contest in their grade. He always did. Noah was the best artist at Littleton Elementary.

"Where are Mom and the Bean?" Charles asked.

"Upstairs. Mom's working on an article and the

Bean's taking a nap." Mrs. Peterson was a reporter for the Littleton newspaper. Lizzie held up a hand. "Toss me one of those grapes."

Charles tossed. Lizzie caught the grape and ate it. *Yum*. "Try getting one in my mouth," she said. She opened wide and Charles lobbed a grape in a high arc. It missed by a mile.

Buddy tried to scramble off Lizzie's lap to chase after the grape. "Oh, no, you don't," said Lizzie, holding him tightly. Maria knelt down to find the grape, which had rolled under the table. Lizzie and Maria had recently learned on the Internet that grapes were not good for dogs.

Just then, the doorbell rang. "Who's *that*?" Lizzie said. Hardly anybody ever used the front door at their house.

"Lizzie, can you see who's there?" Mom called from upstairs.

Lizzie put Buddy down and headed for the door. Buddy followed right at her heels. "You stay inside," she told him, holding him back with her foot as she opened the door.

There on the porch stood Sammy from next door, along with his mom. Sammy was grinning. His mom was not. She was holding a braided leather leash. And at the other end of the leash was a puppy! A panting, pulling puppy. "We just found this guy tied to the apple tree in our front yard," said Sammy's mom. "I think whoever left him didn't have the address quite right," she added. She handed the leash to Lizzie, along with a big white envelope. The envelope was addressed "*To the People Who Take Care of Puppies.*"

CHAPTER TWO

The puppy started to bark and pull at the leash as soon as he saw Lizzie. He had a big, deep bark for such a young dog. He was wagging his little tail so hard that his whole body squirmed. The puppy was white with black spots all over. He had a shiny black nose and deep brown eyes, and he was wearing a bright red collar. "Oh! It's a Dalmatian!" Lizzie dropped to her knees to say hello.

Buddy grabbed his chance and dashed out the door. "Buddy!" Lizzie yelled. She dropped the puppy's leash as she dove for Buddy — and missed.

"Oh, no, you don't!" Sammy grabbed Buddy before he could run off.

"Whew, thanks!" Lizzie said. She whirled around to pick up the puppy's leash, but the little white dog had already charged past her, right through the door and into the house, barking like crazy the whole time.

Yee-haw! Here I am, everybody! Let's play!

"Lizzie?" Mom shouted from upstairs. "What's going on?"

"Tell your mom I said hi," Sammy's mom said quickly. "Gotta go!"

Sammy handed Buddy back to Lizzie. "Good luck," he said with a grin. He followed his mom down the front steps.

Lizzie carried Buddy inside and closed the front door. Then she took Buddy into the den. "Looks like we have a new foster puppy!" she told him. "You're going to stay in here for a minute until I can figure out if he's friendly or not. Be good, okay?" Buddy looked at her quizzically. Lizzie gave him a kiss, put him down, and closed the door behind her. “Maria?” she called over the sound of barking. “Charles?”

“In here,” yelled Maria from the kitchen.

“Help!” yelled Charles.

Lizzie ran into the kitchen to find her best friend and her brother chasing the quick little puppy around the table. “We can’t catch him!” Charles said.

The puppy was barking happily as he careened around the kitchen, slipping and sliding on the floor. His pink tongue was flapping and he was smiling a big goofy doggy smile. It was obvious that he was having the time of his life.

Lizzie started to laugh.

“It’s not funny!” said Maria. “Seriously, we can’t catch him!”

Lizzie ran over to the counter and reached into the doghouse-shaped cookie jar where they kept Buddy’s treats. She pulled out a dog biscuit.

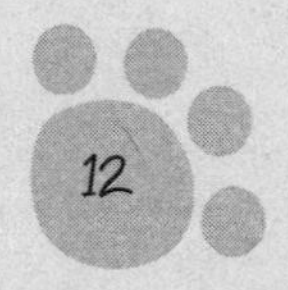

"Here, pup!" she said, holding it out for the puppy to see and smell. "Want a cookie?"

The puppy screeched to a halt under the kitchen table and cocked his head at Lizzie. One ear was black; the other was white. He had one big black spot over his right eye, which made him look absolutely adorable, like a little pirate. "Come on," Lizzie said encouragingly. Slowly, the puppy moved toward her. Charles stepped forward. "Hold on," Lizzie warned. "Don't grab him. That might scare him."

The puppy stretched out his neck and sniffed at the biscuit. "That's it," Lizzie said gently. "Good boy." Slowly, she reached out her other hand and hooked a finger under his collar. Then she let him have the biscuit. The puppy gobbled it down, crunching loudly as crumbs fell to the floor. He put his nose down and snuffled around until he had licked up every scrap with his big pink tongue. Then he looked up at Lizzie and started barking again. His tail was wagging harder than ever.

That was awesome! How about another one — or two?

Lizzie cracked up. This puppy was *trouble* — but he was also very, very cute. Before he could start running around again, she sat down on the floor and pulled him onto her lap for some hugs and kisses.

"What is going *on* here?" Mom was standing in the doorway with her hands on her hips. The Bean stood next to her, holding on to her shirt-tail. He was still rubbing sleep out of his eyes.

The Bean spotted the puppy. "Uppy!" he crowed. He started to run toward Lizzie and the puppy.

"Hold on there, mister!" Mom grabbed the straps of his overalls and hauled him back. "Remember, no patting puppies we don't know."

"But —" the Bean began.

"No buts," Mom said firmly. She lifted the Bean, then turned back to Lizzie and raised an eyebrow. "Where's Buddy? And who, may I ask, is this?" She pointed at the puppy, who was still barking like mad.

"Buddy's in the den," Lizzie said.

"Sammy brought the puppy!" Charles said at the same time. "Somebody dropped him off at their house by mistake."

Mom looked confused. "What?"

"They left this note." Lizzie held up the envelope. She let go of the puppy for a minute. He immediately squirmed out of reach and started running around the kitchen again, slipping and sliding and barking. "Oops," said Lizzie.

Lizzie handed Mom the envelope, brushed a bunch of white hairs off her pants, and then turned to get another biscuit out of the jar. This puppy was going to be a handful! But the Petersons had fostered pesky puppies before. Lizzie wasn't worried. Hadn't they found great homes for

Rascal, the energetic Jack Russell terrier who also barked a lot? And Princess, the most spoiled Yorkshire terrier in the world? And what about Pugsley, also known as Mr. Pest? Lizzie knew she could help this wacky puppy find the perfect home, too.

Mom sat down with the Bean on her lap and opened the envelope. She started to read out loud — *loudly*, so she could be heard over the puppy's barking.

"'This is Cody,'" she read. "'He is six months old. He is a Dalmatian.'"

"I knew that's what he was!" interrupted Lizzie. "Did you know that when Dalmatians are born, they are pure white? They get their spots within a few weeks." Lizzie saw Charles rolling his eyes at Maria. So what? Sometimes Lizzie couldn't help herself. She happened to know a *lot* about dogs. In fact, she had practically memorized her "Dog Breeds of the World" poster. Shouldn't everybody be happy that she was willing to share her knowledge?

"Thank you, Lizzie," said her mom, in a tone that meant "That's enough with the dog facts for now."

"I just think it's important for us to know as much as we can about the dogs we foster," said Lizzie.

"Elizabeth Maude Peterson!" Mom gave her a horrified look. "You can't possibly be thinking that we are going to *foster* this wild puppy!"

CHAPTER THREE

"Of *course* that's what I'm thinking!" said Lizzie. "Mom! C'mon! We *have* to foster this puppy!" She looked at the puppy's adorable face and smiled. Cody the cutie.

Mom sighed. "Couldn't he go to Caring Paws?"

Caring Paws was the animal shelter where Lizzie volunteered one day a week. The people there took care of lots of dogs and cats that needed homes. "No way," Lizzie said, shaking her head. "They're totally full." She wondered if Maria and Charles could see the crossed fingers she was holding behind her back. She wasn't *lying*, exactly. The shelter *was* full. There wasn't a single cage open for another dog, or even a cat.

But the *whole* truth was that Ms. Dobbins, the

director of Caring Paws, would never turn away an animal in need. "We can always find room for one more, if we really have to," she would say.

Mom didn't need to hear that right now. Instead, Lizzie thought Mom needed to hear how important it was for the Petersons to help this puppy. "Somebody wanted *our family* to take care of Cody," Lizzie said. "After all, they left him for *us*, with that note. Read some more! Maybe it will explain why he's here."

Cody barked, as if in agreement.

Mom sighed again and looked at the note. "'Cody is a great dog but way too much of a handful for us,'" she read. "'We did our best but maybe we are just not puppy people. We know you will find him a home with a family who will appreciate Cody's energy.'"

Cody barked some more when he heard his name.

That's me! Cody!

"'P.S.,'" Mom went on reading the note. "'He sheds like crazy. He barks a lot. Also, he pulls on the leash.'"

"No kidding," said Charles.

"'We don't know how to make him stop,'" Mom finished reading. "'Maybe you do.'"

"I do!" Lizzie said. "I mean, I can't make him stop shedding." Lizzie knew that shedding was when a dog's dead hairs fell out all over the place, making a mess. "But I bet anything I can teach Cody to behave!" At that moment, Cody jumped up and put both front paws on the kitchen counter. He sniffed at a loaf of Dad's homemade bread that was sitting out to cool. "Down, Cody!" said Lizzie. The spotted pup dropped back to all fours. "See?" Lizzie was beaming — until she realized that Cody had grabbed a hunk of bread and was gobbling it down.

The Bean was laughing, but Mom frowned. "We don't even know if he and Buddy would get along," she said.

"Please, Mom?" Lizzie asked. "Can't we just give it a try?" Lizzie had just gotten a new puppy-training book out of the library. She was dying to experiment with some of the ideas she had been learning about teaching naughty puppies to behave. Cody would be a really big challenge — but Lizzie liked a challenge. Especially one that had to do with dogs.

And — who could say? — if she could teach Cody to behave, maybe he could even become part of the Peterson family, the way Buddy had! Cody was so cute and so smart. He was going to be a very good dog someday. Lizzie could tell.

"I'll help," promised Charles.

"I'll help, too!" said Maria. "And he's so adorable. I bet you won't have any trouble finding a good home for him."

"I help!" shouted the Bean.

They all turned to look at Cody. He had run completely out of steam and was lying curled up on the red rug by the sink, snoozing. His big paws, with their velvety-soft pink pads, twitched as if he were still running around the kitchen in his dreams. "Awww!" said Lizzie. "Just like Buddy. He plays and plays and then all of a sudden it's nap time."

Cody opened one eye. He really was very, very cute. Especially now that he had stopped barking.

"Well," Mom said. "Let's see what your dad says when he gets home."

"Yay!" yelled Charles and Lizzie and Maria.

"That doesn't mean 'yes,'" Mom warned.

But Lizzie and Charles couldn't help smiling at each other. They knew that now there was a very good chance they would get to foster Cody.

"Hey, where's the Bean?" Lizzie asked, suddenly realizing that her little brother had not joined in the cheering.

The Bean had wriggled off Mom's lap and wandered away. Now he charged back into the kitchen, with Buddy romping alongside him. "See if they friends!" he said.

The Bean had let Buddy out of the den. He must have heard Mom wondering if Cody and Buddy would get along. Lizzie groaned. The Bean was just trying to be helpful, but this could be trouble!

Lizzie barely had time to worry. Cody woke quickly from his nap and jumped right up to play with Buddy. The two puppies sniffed at each other and wagged their tails, then immediately started to chase each other around the kitchen. Now *two* dogs were barking their heads off.

Mom put her hands over her ears. But she was smiling. "Dad's sure going to get a big surprise when he gets home tonight," she said.

Mr. Peterson was working late because the fire station was having an open house for some of the elderly people who lived at a place called The Meadows. The Littleton fire department liked to have people come visit, especially during Fire Prevention Week.

Dad got home just in time for supper. Lizzie and Charles met him at the door and pulled him inside, talking about Cody the whole time. "Please, Dad?" Lizzie begged. "Can we foster him?"

"Well, hey there, little guy!" Dad said, kneeling down to take a look at Cody, who was zonked out again. This time he was sleeping on the living room rug, in front of the fireplace. He and Buddy had curled up together after a long afternoon of play.

"That's Cody," Lizzie said.

At the sound of his name, Cody woke up fast. He jumped to his feet and started barking at Dad.

Uh-oh. Lizzie held her breath.

But Dad just laughed. "Welcome, Cody!" he said.

CHAPTER FOUR

"Wait up, Cody! Slow down! Stop pulling!" Lizzie ran after the spotted dog, who was dragging her along as he snuffled and sniffed and checked out every single object along the sidewalk. For a little dog, he was really strong.

Wow! Smell this! Incredible! And what about this? Is this something to eat? I'm so excited to have a new place to explore!

Once Mom and Dad had agreed to let Cody stay for a while, Lizzie had stayed up late reading her puppy training book. Now it was Saturday, which was Lizzie's usual day at Caring Paws. But Lizzie wasn't going to the animal shelter. When

Ms. Dobbins had heard about the new puppy, she had told Lizzie to take the day off "to get to know the little guy." So instead, Lizzie and Cody were on their way to Maria's house.

"My mom said she wants to meet Cody," Maria had said, when she called that morning. "Plus, she thinks maybe Simba could be a good influence on him. Simba is such a mellow guy."

Maria's mom was blind, and Simba, a big yellow Lab, was her guide dog. He was always very calm, often falling fast asleep while he lay at his owner's feet waiting for his next assignment. But the second that Mrs. Santiago stood up, Simba would jump up, too. Simba was always ready to work. He went everywhere with Maria's mom: to the grocery store, to the doctor, even to restaurants. And he always had perfect doggy manners: He did not sniff people, or jump up on them, or bark. Lizzie agreed that he would be a very good role model for Cody.

Lizzie and Maria were planning to work on

their Halloween costumes and also get started on Cody's training. "Since he's so young, we should only work with him for ten minutes at a time," Lizzie reminded Maria. "A puppy can't pay attention for too much longer than that. So we'll have plenty of time between training sessions."

"We have *got* to teach you to stop pulling," Lizzie told the happy pup as she rang Maria's doorbell. She shook out her arm. It was sore from hanging on to Cody! The puppy grinned back at her and wagged all over.

Sure! Whatever you say!

Maria's mom answered the door. Simba stood next to her. When the big dog spotted Lizzie, he wagged his tail. But Lizzie didn't pet Simba. She knew she wasn't supposed to distract a guide dog who was on the job.

"Hi, Mrs. Santiago," she said. "This is Cody!"

Cody barked to say hello.

Maria's mom reached down to touch the puppy. "My, his fur is so soft!" she said. "And his little body feels strong. He must be a healthy boy."

"He is," said Lizzie. "He's absolutely perfect — well, except for the barking and the pulling and the shedding."

"He'll grow out of most of that," predicted Mrs. Santiago. "He's just a puppy."

Simba stepped forward to sniff Cody. Cody jumped up and started biting at Simba's neck, but Simba just shook him off.

"Maria's upstairs in her room," said Mrs. Santiago. "She has all her art supplies out. Have fun making your costumes!"

Cody dragged Lizzie up the stairs and straight into Maria's room. Maria pulled Cody onto her bed for a big kiss and hug hello, while Lizzie looked around at the mess of paints, markers, glue pens, and other art supplies. "I have the coolest costume idea!" Maria told Lizzie. "Look, Dad found these huge cardboard tubes." She pointed to two garbage-can-sized cylinders standing in the corner of her room. "They're big enough for us to wear!"

"Uh-huh," Lizzie said. "So — what's your idea?"

"We can paint them!" Maria said. "We could be soda cans, or soup, or — anything!"

Lizzie considered this. It wasn't a bad idea. In fact, she wished *she* had thought of it. But soup cans? That seemed kind of boring. Not that she would say so out loud. Lately Lizzie had been working hard at keeping her opinions to herself. She gazed at the tubes. "I've got it!" she said. "P.B. and J.! We'll paint the tubes to look like jars of peanut butter and jelly!"

Maria laughed. "Perfect," she said. "I bet you want to be peanut butter, right?"

"I don't even care." Lizzie looked down at Cody, who had decided it was time for a snooze. He was curled up nose-to-tail on Maria's bed, with the baby-pink bottoms of his paws showing. "Awww! We can't train him if he's sleeping, so we might as well get started on our costumes. Let's practice painting the labels on a piece of paper first," she suggested.

They flipped a coin to see who got to be peanut butter (Lizzie won), stuck a CD into Maria's player, and got to work. Lizzie had not done any painting in a long time, and it was so much fun that she almost forgot about Cody. Almost — until, between songs on the CD, she heard a crunching, tearing noise from behind her.

"Oh, no!" she cried, when she turned to look. Cody must have woken up a while ago, because he was already well into destroying the *second* cardboard tube. For a moment, Lizzie was mad. But Cody looked so innocent and so cute, sitting there surrounded by shredded cardboard. She just started laughing, and Maria joined in.

"I guess that's the end of *that* costume idea," Lizzie said, crumpling up her painting. "Oh, well! We might as well do some training."

"What are we going to teach him first?" Maria asked.

"Mom says we have *got* to get him to stop barking so much, so that's top priority," said Lizzie. "This book had a great way to do it. First we put him in a situation where he'll bark — like, if you go out in the hall and then knock on the door."

"Okay," said Maria. "Then what?"

"Well," Lizzie explained, "most dog owners start yelling at the dog to be quiet, but that never works. The dog just thinks they're barking along with him. Instead, I'm going to wait until he stops barking for even a *second*, and then say 'Good boy!' and give him a treat. After a few times, I'll say 'Quiet!' when he stops barking, and if we repeat the whole thing about a billion times, he *might* learn to stop barking when I say 'Quiet.'" It had sounded pretty easy in the book, but now Lizzie wasn't so sure.

Maria went out in the hall and closed the door. A few seconds later, she knocked. Cody exploded into loud woofs. Lizzie waited and waited, but the puppy barely seemed to take a breath. Finally, Cody stopped to look up at Lizzie, his head cocked to one side.

What's going on? Isn't there somebody at the door?

"Good boy!" Lizzie said. She pulled a tiny biscuit ("small, one-gulp treats are best for training," the book had said) out of her pocket and popped it into Cody's mouth.

He swallowed it right down and instantly started barking again. Lizzie could see that training Cody was going to take a while.

CHAPTER FIVE

"Ha-ha! Well, hang in there. I'm sure he'll get the idea sooner or later!" Chief Olson laughed some more. "Those Dalmatians. They sure are energetic when they're pups!"

It was later that same week, and the entire fourth grade of Littleton Elementary was at the firehouse for a tour. All the grades had been going over, and now it was finally their turn. The other kids were milling around in the firehouse lobby while they waited for their tour to begin, punching one another and giggling when their teachers told them to settle down. But Lizzie was talking to Chief Olson. She was telling him all about Cody and his mischievous ways. She knew he would be interested: Chief Olson owned the firehouse mascot, a Dalmatian named Gunnar.

Lizzie had known Gunnar for a long time. He was the best-behaved dog she had ever met — plus, he was a hero. Gunnar had once pulled someone out of a burning building. He had saved a life! "You're amazing, Gunnar," said Lizzie, giving the big dog's solid shoulder a pat. Gunnar sat quietly next to the chief, wearing a more mature version of Cody's goofy smile. Gunnar was always on hand to welcome groups who were touring the firehouse.

"Is Gunnar going to be riding with us in the parade?" Lizzie asked Chief Olson.

"You bet he is!" The chief grinned. "He wouldn't miss it for the world."

Lizzie petted Gunnar again. It was hard to imagine that Cody would ever grow up to be as calm as this. Not that he wasn't learning! Lizzie was still practicing with him every day, and sometimes Cody would stop barking for as long as five seconds after she had told him "Quiet." Next Lizzie planned to start teaching Cody how to sit and wait when she opened the front door, instead of jumping up excitedly. Then maybe she could figure out how to teach him to quit pulling on the leash.

"Okay, we're all set!" Lizzie's dad stepped in front of the crowd of kids. "Hello, fourth graders! I'm firefighter Paul — otherwise known as Lizzie's dad." He winked at Lizzie and smiled around at the crowd. "Welcome to you all. How many of you have been to the firehouse before?"

Lots of kids raised their hands, including Lizzie.

"I remember when we came here in kindergarten," yelled out Daniel, a boy in Lizzie's class. "Jessica cried when she saw the fireman in his oxygen mask and everything."

Jessica punched Daniel. "Shut up!" She was blushing.

"That happens sometimes," said Lizzie's father.

"Little kids can be afraid of things that are strange to them. That's why we let them see what a firefighter looks like, all dressed up in gear. If you're five years old and your house is on fire, you need to know that the firefighter is your friend, no matter how scary he or she looks."

Caroline raised her hand. "I remember in second grade when we got to climb onto the truck," she said. "That was exciting when we were little." Lizzie saw that she was gazing wistfully at the big ladder truck.

Lizzie's dad smiled. "Kids of *all* ages like to do that," he said. "We'll get a chance after we tour the building. But before we do that," he said, "let's play a little game. How long do you think it will take me to get into my firefighting gear?"

"A minute!" yelled out Noah.

Everybody else started shouting at the same time. "Five minutes!" "Three seconds!" "Four hours!"

Lizzie's dad laughed at that last one. "Who has

a watch? You can time me." He walked over to the rack where all the firefighters' gear was stored. "Ready? Here I go!" He jumped into his boots, then pulled up his baggy pants, stretching the suspenders over his shoulders. He buttoned the pants, pulled on a fire-retardant hood, slipped into his heavy jacket, pulled on a pair of gloves, and plopped his helmet on top of his head. "Stop! How long was that?"

Daniel checked his watch. "Wow!" he said. "Twenty-five seconds."

Lizzie knew her dad's record was twenty-one, but she cheered along with everyone else. Then she and the rest of the fourth graders followed him upstairs, checking out the bunkroom, the offices, the kitchen, and the room where all the firefighters hung out, playing cards or reading when they weren't busy. Mr. Peterson explained about all the chores they had to do: cleaning the firehouse and the equipment, cooking, fixing anything that was broken. "It's a lot of work," said

Lizzie's dad. "But this is our house, and we have to take care of it."

When it was time to go downstairs, Lizzie's dad asked, "Anyone want to see me slide down the pole?"

"Yeah!" everybody yelled.

They all trooped down the stairs and waited at the bottom. In a second, Mr. Peterson came sliding down the pole with a big grin on his face. "Yahoo!" he yelled. Everybody cracked up. They could all tell what Lizzie knew: that her Dad *loved* that part of being a firefighter. Lizzie smiled at him, feeling proud enough to burst.

"Okay, on to the trucks," said Mr. Peterson, leading the way. "You can each climb up into the driver's seat of the ladder truck and see how it feels to sit there. Chief will help you down on the other side when you're done."

It happened when Lizzie was waiting for her turn.

A loud bell started clanging and a voice came

over the loudspeaker. "Possible heart attack at Thirty-two Elm Street. All units respond."

All the firefighters were also emergency medical technicians. They rode the ambulance whenever and wherever they were needed. Three guys and a woman came sliding down the pole, one after another, dressed in their blue EMT coveralls. They ran to the ambulance that was parked next to the fire truck and jumped in.

"Gunnar, out of the way!" yelled Chief Olson. Lizzie saw that Gunnar was sitting right in front of the ambulance, facing the other direction.

"Gunnar!" yelled the chief again.

The big rig's engine started to rumble and the giant garage door began to rise.

But Gunnar did not move.

CHAPTER SIX

"So then what happened?" Ms. Dobbins asked. It was a few days after the firehouse visit and Lizzie was at Caring Paws. She hated to leave Cody, but she didn't want to miss another Saturday of volunteering at the animal shelter.

Now Lizzie was telling Ms. Dobbins about what had happened with Gunnar, while they cleaned out a cage in the dog room. Ozzie, a beagle who had been staying at Caring Paws, had just been adopted. It was time to get his cage ready for the next dog who might need it. The other dogs in the room had barked like crazy when Ms. Dobbins and Lizzie first came in, but by now they had calmed down.

"It was so weird, because Gunnar *always*

behaves. But this time it seemed like he was not listening. He just sat there, staring into space! Finally, Chief Olson went over and grabbed him by the collar. He had to pull Gunnar out of the way so the ambulance could go." Lizzie frowned, remembering.

"Was the chief angry?" asked Ms. Dobbins.

"No." It made Lizzie sad to think about it. "He wasn't mad at all. He just kept shaking his head. And then he told me that Gunnar is going deaf."

"Oh, dear," said Ms. Dobbins. She handed Lizzie a squeaky toy, a red water dish, and a green fleecy blanket. They would all have to be washed for the next dog. "That's too bad. But lots of dogs lose at least some of their hearing as they age. It's not too hard to teach them hand signals for things like 'sit' and 'come.'"

"That's cool," Lizzie said. "And Gunnar's so smart! I bet he could learn those really fast."

Now Ms. Dobbins was sloshing soapy water from a bucket onto the cage's cement floor.

"Although," she said thoughtfully, "I suppose that might not be enough for a firehouse dog."

Lizzie sighed. "You're right. That's the problem. Chief Olson said that it just wasn't safe anymore for Gunnar to roam all over the firehouse. He's going to have to stay in the office from now on, or at home." She knew her dad and the other firefighters would really miss having Gunnar around. They liked to brush him, or play tug with him, or slip him treats from the fridge.

"Did you know that some Dalmatians are *born* deaf?" Ms. Dobbins asked. She reached out a hand for the mop that Lizzie was holding.

Lizzie handed it over. "Really?" This was an interesting new dog fact!

Ms. Dobbins nodded. "Some people think it has something to do with their white coloring. White animals often have hearing problems, especially those with blue eyes. Remember that white cat we had in here for a long time? Daisy? She was a little deaf."

Lizzie could picture Daisy, a big cat with a rumbly purr and a long white coat. She'd had one blue eye and one green one. "So do you think Gunnar is deaf because he is a Dalmatian?"

Ms. Dobbins shook her head. "No, in his case it's probably just that he is getting older." She finished mopping the floor and handed the mop back to Lizzie. "There. All done." She brushed off her hands. "So, how's that little Cody doing?"

"Better," Lizzie reported. "He seems to understand what I mean by 'Quiet' even if he doesn't always obey. But he's still pretty wild. The worst part is how he pulls on the leash when you walk him. It's driving us all crazy! Mom thinks we should try one of those prong collars, but I think they look like they would hurt the dog's neck."

"I know just what you need," said Ms. Dobbins. "Have you met our newest shelter dog, Roscoe?"

"Not yet," said Lizzie. "I've heard about him. He's a big Rottweiler, right?"

"Big? He's huge!" Ms. Dobbins laughed. "He's

like a truck." She put away the mop and bucket and started walking toward the back of the dog room. "Come on, I'll introduce you."

"Wow!" Lizzie stared into cage number three. Roscoe was a very impressive dog. He was brown and black, with muscles like a bodybuilder, a gigantic, blocky head, and paws the size of hamburgers. Lizzie was not afraid of dogs, but she could imagine that *some* people might be frightened by Roscoe.

"He's very gentle." Ms. Dobbins seemed to read Lizzie's mind. "Wouldn't hurt a flea. But he sure can pull when he's on a leash!"

Lizzie felt a twinge in her shoulder. If little *Cody's* pulling had made her sore, how could she handle Roscoe? One of her jobs at the shelter was exercising the dogs. But how would she ever be able to hang on to this big boy?

"That's why we use one of these," Ms. Dobbins said, showing Lizzie a tangle of red nylon webbing that was clipped to the front of Roscoe's cage.

"It's a head halter." She opened Roscoe's cage door and stepped inside. "It goes over his nose, and you clip the leash just under his jaw." She demonstrated as she was talking. "Now you can walk him easily. It works by putting just a little bit of pressure on his nose, which is very sensitive. Even a little tug on the leash will remind him not to pull."

Roscoe pawed at the halter.

"It's a little itchy," Ms. Dobbins explained as she came out of the cage with Roscoe on the leash. "But it doesn't hurt him or anything. He'll get used to it soon." She handed the leash to Lizzie. "Go ahead, take him outside. You'll see how it works."

Lizzie gave Roscoe a pat. "Hello, Roscoe," she said. "I'm Lizzie. Want to go for a walk?" Roscoe stopped pawing at the halter. His ears pricked up and his stumpy tail started to wag. He looked happily at Lizzie. "Good dog! Let's go!" Lizzie led him toward the back door that opened into the exercise yard.

It was amazing! Roscoe didn't pull at all. And when Lizzie wanted him to stop sniffing at a certain patch of grass, all she had to do was give the leash a tiny tug, just as Ms. Dobbins had said. The head harness was like magic!

"Do you happen to have one of those things in Cody's size?" Lizzie asked Ms. Dobbins, when she had finished walking Roscoe. Lizzie's mom would be arriving any minute to drive her home, where Cody was probably due for a walk himself.

"I had a feeling you'd ask that." Ms. Dobbins held out a smaller green version of Roscoe's harness. "Good luck!"

"Thanks! I'll need it," said Lizzie. "I have a feeling it's going to take more than a head harness to tame Cody."

Ms. Dobbins nodded. "You know what would be best for him? To be adopted by someone who also owns an older, calmer dog. I think your wild Cody needs a role model."

Lizzie remembered Maria's mom saying the

same thing, about how a dog like Simba would be a good influence on Cody. But Simba was a working dog! He didn't have time to teach a young pup how to act. Then Lizzie thought of another dog she knew, a dog who was just as calm and mature as Simba. Lizzie's eyes met Ms. Dobbins's. "Are you thinking what I'm thinking?" she asked.

CHAPTER SEVEN

"It's perfect!" said Lizzie. "It's like it was meant to be. Cody *belongs* there. I mean, he's a Dalmatian! It's tradition!" Lizzie had been reading all about Dalmatians and their history as "carriage dogs," who ran alongside horse-drawn fire trucks.

"They'll all love him!" Maria predicted. "Especially now that he's so much better behaved. That shows how well he can learn!"

Cody had learned so much, so quickly. Lizzie could hardly believe it! A little over a week ago Cody had appeared on the Petersons' doorstep, a barking, pulling, jumping bundle of energy. And today, here he was, trotting down the sidewalk between Lizzie and Maria like a perfect little gentleman. The head harness worked perfectly! Cody was a different puppy already. Lizzie would have loved to keep him forever, but by now she knew her mom would not agree to that. Mom liked Cody, but she did *not* like the way he shed little white hairs all over everything.

It was time to introduce Cody to the man who Lizzie and Maria — and Ms. Dobbins — believed would be the perfect owner for him. Who else but Chief Olson?

For one thing, Lizzie knew the chief was really going to miss having Gunnar at his side every minute of every day at the firehouse.

For another, she knew that the chief loved Dalmatians — and understood them, too! He would know just what to expect: the energy, the shedding, all of it — unlike the people who had given up Cody.

And finally, Cody would grow up with one of the world's best dogs — Gunnar — as a teacher and friend.

"Maybe one day you'll be a hero, too!" Lizzie told the prancing, spotted dog. Cody grinned up at her.

Sure, whatever! This is fun! I don't know where we're going, but I can't wait to get there!

"Did you call Chief Olson to let him know we were coming?" Maria asked.

Lizzie shook her head. "No, and I told Dad not to tell him, either. I want to surprise the chief. He is not going to *believe* how much Cody has already learned."

It took twice as long as usual to walk to the firehouse, since it seemed like everybody they passed just had to stop the girls so they could pat Cody and ask a million questions about the puppy. Cody had such a great personality! Everybody loved him.

When the girls finally rounded the corner near the firehouse, Cody pricked up his ears and sniffed

the air. For a moment, he strained at the leash — until Lizzie gave him a little tug to remind him not to pull. "I bet he smells Gunnar!" Lizzie said.

Cody did not hesitate when Lizzie pushed open the firehouse door. He pranced inside as if he already belonged there, tail high and ears on alert.

"Hey, look who's here!" Lizzie's dad called out. "Cody! My man!" He knelt down and opened his arms, and Cody ran to him, wriggling with happiness. He gave Mr. Peterson lots of sloppy kisses with his big pink tongue.

"Ooh, who's this cutie?" asked Meg, a firefighter Lizzie knew well. Meg had adopted Scout, a German shepherd that the Petersons had fostered. Scout was training to be a search-and-rescue dog. Meg knelt down for kisses, too.

Soon Cody was surrounded by firefighters. He loved all the attention. The spotted pup gave big kisses to everyone who came over to hug and pat him.

This is the greatest! All these people love me — and I love them, too!

Suddenly, Lizzie's dad jumped to his feet. "Oh — hey, Chief!" he said. "We were just —"

Chief Olson had appeared. He was standing there, watching. He had a funny happy-sad expression on his face, and Gunnar waited quietly by his side. "This can't be the wild young pup I've been hearing about!" he said. "He looks pretty well-behaved to me."

Gunnar stepped forward, and he and Cody touched noses. Gunnar's tail was wagging.

"Gunnar likes him!" said Lizzie. "That's perfect, because —"

Maria punched Lizzie in the arm. Their plan had been to let Chief Olson think it was all *his* idea to adopt Cody.

". . . because it's great when dogs get along," Lizzie finished lamely.

Chief Olson didn't seem to notice. He had knelt down to tousle Cody's ears. "Well, aren't you a good-looking fellow," he said. "Healthy, strong —"

"And really smart!" Lizzie couldn't help putting in. She didn't care if Maria punched her again. "You wouldn't believe all the things he's already learned!"

"So he's a quick study, is he?" asked the chief, looking thoughtful. He watched as Gunnar let Cody chew on his ear for a while before firmly batting the pesky pup away. "And you're trying to find him a home?"

Lizzie couldn't stand it one second longer. "Yes!" she said. "With you!"

Maria threw up her hands, laughing.

The chief was laughing, too. "As a matter of fact, that's exactly what I was thinking. I have a feeling Gunnar would really like to show this pup the ropes. It would give our old boy something to do, a job. And I can see that Cody here will make a great firehouse mascot when he's all grown up." The chief stood up and looked around at the other firefighters. "What do you all think?"

"Yes!" everybody yelled at once. Dad gave Lizzie a big high five.

Maria and Lizzie stood grinning at each other. Then Lizzie felt something tugging on her foot. "Cody!" she cried. "Quit eating my shoelaces!"

Everybody cracked up.

Lizzie and Maria headed home a little while later, with Cody walking perfectly on the leash. They were feeling happy and proud. "Mom will be so impressed that we already found a home for Cody!" Lizzie was saying as they passed the post office.

Just then, a woman who was walking in the other direction suddenly stopped. "Did I hear you call that dog Cody?" she asked.

Lizzie and Maria stopped, too. Cody sat back on his little butt and looked up at the woman. He didn't bark or pull on the leash. The woman, who was very thin with a sort of pinched-up face, reached down to pet him, but Cody ducked his head.

"That's his name," Lizzie said. "Do you know him?"

The woman looked confused and started talking fast. "Um — I think I used to know a puppy by that name," she said. "But — it must have been another Cody. He looked like this puppy, but he sure acted different." Then she walked off quickly, before Lizzie could say another word.

"Who was that?" asked Maria.

"I don't know," said Lizzie. She looked down at Cody, who was still sitting very quietly as he watched the woman walk away. "But I have a feeling Cody does."

CHAPTER EIGHT

That night, after dinner, Lizzie and her family sat in the living room, eating apple pie with vanilla ice cream, a special dessert to celebrate Cody's good luck in finding a home with Chief Olson. Lizzie wished she could forget about what had happened earlier that day. Who *was* that woman who had stopped Lizzie and Maria on the street? And why did she seem to recognize Cody? Lizzie could not stop wondering — and worrying. Somehow she just had a bad feeling about the whole thing. But she was trying not to let it ruin Cody's last night at the Petersons'.

"Sit!" The Bean was standing by the fireplace. Cody stood in front of him, wagging his tail. The Bean held up a finger. "Tody, sit!"

Cody did not sit. He stood there with his head cocked to one side. He barked a few times.

That word sounds sort of familiar. I think this small person wants me to do something. But what? Maybe he wants me to bark.

"Sit!" the Bean said again, in a stern, deep voice like the one Dad used when he wanted Buddy to do something.

Cody barked again and wagged his tail harder.

"Sit!" the Bean said, in the happy voice Lizzie used for training. "Sit, sit, sit, sit, sit!" he pleaded. "Please?"

Lizzie laughed. She put down her dessert bowl and swooped the Bean up in her arms. "Are you training Cody?" she asked. The Bean nodded, with his lip stuck way far out. Lizzie knew he was just trying to copy what he had seen her do many, many times a day ever since Cody had come to stay. It took a lot of work to train a puppy! She knew how frustrating it could be.

"But the uppy won't sit!" the Bean wailed.

"Here's what you have to do," Lizzie said, setting the Bean back down on his feet. "Cody," she said, turning to the spotted pup. "Sit!" She touched Cody's back lightly, just enough to remind him of what it was she wanted him to do.

Oh, I get it! You want me to sit! That's easy!

Cody plopped his little butt down and grinned up at Lizzie. "Good boy!" she said, laughing. "See, he's just starting to learn what that word means," she told her little brother. "Sometimes he needs a little help remembering."

The Bean threw his arms around Cody and hugged him. "I love you, Tody," he said.

Lizzie knew her whole family was going to miss having Cody around.

Suddenly, Dad slapped his forehead. "I almost

forgot!" He went to rummage in the pocket of the jacket he'd been wearing that day and came back carrying a little red rubber fire hydrant. "Chief sent this chew toy home with me, to give to Cody," he said. "It used to be Gunnar's." He gave the toy to Cody, who immediately lay down and started chewing on it. When Buddy tried to steal it, Cody picked it up and ran behind Mom's easy chair.

Then Charles went upstairs and came back with a play firefighter's helmet. He and Lizzie put it on Cody's head, adjusting the elastic strap under his jaw.

"Oh, he is *so* cute!" said Lizzie. "Quick! Quick! Somebody get the camera!" Lizzie couldn't believe how sweet Cody looked in his fire hat, one big spotted paw holding the squeaking fire hydrant down so he could gnaw on it with his sharp white puppy teeth. Mom ran for the camera, and they snapped picture after picture. Everybody laughed when Buddy tried to steal the fire hydrant again. This time he managed to grab it, and the two puppies zoomed around the room wrestling and growling and tugging over the new toy. Cody's fire hat got knocked sideways, making him look cuter than ever.

A few moments later, the puppies were all tired out. Cody was snoozing on the rug, all curled up with Buddy. Lizzie could not help sighing as she looked at their cute, sleepy faces. Cody's fire hat had finally fallen all the way off and Buddy was lying on it. One part of Cody's lip was tucked up over a tooth, giving him a goofy look. They were so adorable together. Lizzie wished Cody could just stay with the Petersons, but she knew he would be happy with the chief. Being a firehouse dog was really something special.

Mom had put the Bean to bed. Now she came back into the room and saw that the puppies were sleeping. "How about a game of Scrabble?" she asked.

"But Scrabble is so —" Lizzie slapped a hand over her own mouth, before the rest of the sentence could come out. "Boring!" was the word she swallowed. Scrabble *was* boring, at least in Lizzie's opinion. It was almost as boring as Candy Land, which the Bean liked to play over and over and over. But she had to admit it was just her opinion. She knew that not everybody agreed with her about Scrabble — although she was pretty sure Charles did, from the look on his face.

Just then, the phone rang. "I'll get it!" Lizzie sprang to her feet, happy to have something else to do. Cody jumped up, too, and started to bark. "Quiet!" Lizzie said. Cody stopped for a second, just long enough for Lizzie to say, "Good boy!" and give him a pat. Then he barked a few more times as he padded after her into the kitchen, where she picked up the phone.

"Hello?"

"Hello, is this — is this the little girl I saw today, with the Dalmatian?"

Lizzie frowned. Right away, she recognized the voice of the pinched-face woman. "This is Lizzie Peterson," she said.

"Lizzie Peterson," the woman repeated. "And your family fosters puppies, right?"

"That's right."

"And somebody gave you that Dalmatian to foster a little while ago?"

"That's right," Lizzie said again. She was about to mention that the "somebody" had gone off and left Cody tied up — at the wrong house! — but the woman interrupted.

"My husband would like to speak to you."

By now, Mom had come into the kitchen. She gave Lizzie a raised-eyebrow look that meant "Who is it?"

Lizzie just shrugged and shook her head.

"Hello?" said a man's voice on the phone. "I'm Tim Stone. And that Dalmatian you have? That's our dog. Cody."

Lizzie drew in a breath. She didn't say a word. How *dare* these people, who had abandoned Cody, call him their dog?

"We couldn't handle him, but my wife tells me that you can," the man went on. "She said he was like a different dog, walking so nicely on the leash, and hardly barking at all."

"*Anybody* can handle Cody, now that I trained him!" Lizzie burst out.

"If that's true," the man said, "we want our puppy back."

CHAPTER NINE

Without a word, Lizzie handed her mother the phone. She could not believe this was happening!

"This is Betsy Peterson," Mom said into the phone. "And to whom am I speaking?"

Lizzie could never have been so polite! In fact, she couldn't even stand to listen to the rest of the conversation. She went back into the living room, with Cody following her. Then she sat down by the fire, pulled Cody onto her lap, and kissed the top of his head.

"Who was that on the phone?" Dad asked.

Lizzie just buried her face in Cody's neck. She couldn't seem to say a thing.

A few moments later, Mom came back into the room. "Well!" she said. "This is a new twist."

"What is going *on*?" asked Dad.

"That was the people who used to own Cody," Mom said. "Tim and Cheryl Stone. I guess Mrs. Stone saw Cody downtown with Lizzie and Maria today" — she glanced at Lizzie, who nodded miserably — "and, well, now they want him back."

"What?" Charles looked shocked. "Why?" Buddy, who had been sleeping on Charles's lap, woke up for a second and looked around.

"Well, because now he can walk on a leash, and he doesn't bark all the time. They think they might be able to handle Cody after all." Mom sighed. "They miss him."

"I can understand that," Dad said slowly. "He's a lovable pup. But —"

"I know," Mom said. "What about Chief Olson? I explained that we had already found a great new home for Cody. But they insisted on coming over to talk about it."

Lizzie hugged Cody closer. "When?" was all she said.

"They live just over on Foster Street. They'll be here any minute." Mom looked around at all the unhappy faces. "What could I say? Maybe they have a right to take Cody back. After all, he was their dog first."

"But —" Lizzie began.

The doorbell rang before she could say another word. Buddy and Cody started to bark. Lizzie told them "Quiet!" and they both stopped.

Mom gave Lizzie a stern look. "Let's just hear these people out," she said. "It's only fair."

Lizzie did not agree. She didn't think there was one fair thing about the whole situation. But she could see that once again she was going to have to keep her opinion to herself. Anyway, Mom had left to answer the door.

"Come on into the living room," Lizzie heard Mom say. And then, there she was — the pinched-face woman. She was wearing an orange sweater with a jack-o'-lantern face on it. With her was a man whose face was not pinched at all — in fact, it was round and pink.

"Tim Stone," he said, in a big, booming voice. He smiled a broad smile as he held out his hand to Dad for a shake. Then he turned and saw the spotted pup in Lizzie's lap. "Cody!" he boomed. "Come here, boy!"

Lizzie remembered how Cody had ducked when the woman had tried to pet him on the street, so she was not at all surprised when the puppy did not jump up and run to Tim Stone.

Tim Stone came over and scratched behind Cody's ears. "There's my boy!" He held out his arms and Lizzie felt like she had to hand Cody over, even though she hated to. Tim Stone cradled Cody awkwardly for a moment, then handed him to his wife. She held the puppy gingerly, as if trying to avoid getting his white hairs on her sweater.

"I guess we'll take him on home, then," said Tim Stone, with the same big smile.

"No way!" Lizzie burst out. She could not help herself. She knew nobody had asked her, but she had a definite opinion about all of this and she was not about to keep it to herself. "First of all, you gave Cody up! You *abandoned* him, just because he barked and pulled on the leash and shed hair all over the place. Now he doesn't bark as much, and he's learning not to pull, but he still sheds, and he's still a puppy. A puppy who's going to chew things, and make mistakes, and — and what are you going to do the first time he misbehaves? Abandon him again?"

Dad cleared his throat. Lizzie wondered if he was going to tell her to tone it down, but instead he faced the Stones. "You know, Lizzie has a point. We might need to think about this," he began.

"What's there to think about?" Tim Stone pulled some papers out of his pocket. "Cody is ours. We can prove it! Here's the receipt from the pet store where we bought him. He wasn't cheap, either."

Dad nodded. "I understand. But we thought

this puppy needed a home, and we found him a good one. As a foster family, that's what we do. You gave him up, and now you're saying you want him back. But Chief Olson, my boss down at the firehouse, wants him, too. Perhaps he'd even be willing to give you the money you paid for Cody, I don't know. Anyway, we will have to think about what's best for Cody." He got up and took Cody out of Cheryl's arms. "Thank you for coming by."

Cheryl and Tim Stone did not look happy. But Dad was not backing down. He brought Cody to Lizzie and placed the sleepy little puppy carefully into her arms. Then he walked the Stones to the front door and said good night.

CHAPTER TEN

Lizzie looked down at Cody, who was lying in her lap. Then she looked at her parents. "I'm sorry," she said in a small voice.

"Don't be," said Mom. "You were right to speak up."

"Absolutely," Dad agreed. "At first I thought that the right thing to do would be to give Cody back to the Stones. But what you said is true! He *is* still a puppy, and I think they were right in the first place about not being puppy people."

"Did you see how that lady made a face when Cody kissed her?" Charles asked. "They are *definitely* not puppy people."

Lizzie gave the sleepy puppy a squeeze. "But

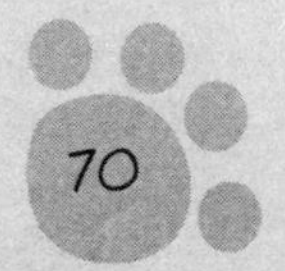

they did pay for Cody," she said. "Can we really say no if they want him back?"

"I'm not sure," Dad said slowly.

Just then, the doorbell rang. Mom raised her eyebrows and went to answer the door. When she came back into the room, the Stones were with her. Lizzie hugged Cody closer. Were they going to insist on taking him right now?

"We didn't even make it all the way home," said Cheryl Stone, all in a rush. "We realized by the time we got to Elm Street that you were one hundred percent right." She was looking straight at Lizzie. "We really didn't mean to abandon him, you know. We thought we were doing the right thing, giving him to your family. But it wasn't right to just leave him and run away. Was it?" she asked her husband, giving him a nudge.

Tim Stone smiled sheepishly. "No," he admitted. "I guess we were just a little overwhelmed by Cody's energy. I think maybe we'll get ourselves a grown dog instead of a puppy."

"Or a cat, even," said Cheryl Stone. "I've always been more of a cat person, really." She and Mom shared a smile.

"What about the money?" Dad asked.

Tim Stone waved a hand. "Why don't we just consider it a donation to the fire station? You people provide a tremendous service for the whole community. It's the least I can do."

"And that," Lizzie told Maria as she finished telling the story the next morning, "was that!" They were walking downtown again, with Cody. Only this time Charles and Sammy and Buddy and the Bean were all with them. And this time Cody was going to the firehouse to stay! First, though, they were all going to be part of the big Halloween parade. Lizzie and Maria had finally come up with the *perfect* costumes for themselves — and for everyone else, too.

It was a crisp, sunny day — just right for a

parade! As they walked, Cody pranced ahead of them all with his head held high.

Oh, boy, oh, boy! I think we're going to that fun place again, with the big dog that looks just like me!

Chief Olson was out in front of the fire station, giving one last polish to the big chrome bumper of his old fire truck. The chief was looking snappy in his navy blue dress uniform, with its shiny brass buttons. "Well, well, well!" he said. "Look who's here!" He knelt right down and opened up his arms, and Cody ran to him. The puppy's tail was wagging like crazy as he licked the chief's face all over. Gunnar walked over and touched noses with Cody, as if to say, "Welcome, little one."

The chief had been totally focused on Cody. But now he looked up at Lizzie, Maria, Charles,

Sammy, and the Bean. He burst into laughter. "Perfect!" he said.

All of them had on white pj's, with black spots painted all over. Lizzie had used Mom's eyebrow pencil to draw whiskers on all their faces, and they all wore funny hats that Mom had found at the variety store, with black spots and floppy ears. They were dressed as Dalmatians, every one of them! Even Buddy had on a little white vest with black spots. And of course Cody didn't need a costume at all. The chief's fire truck would be *full* of Dalmatians!

"And you're right on time," the chief went on. "We're supposed to be heading down to the corner of Main and Broadway. The parade is starting in five minutes!" He helped them all up into his fire truck, carefully placing Cody onto Lizzie's lap and Buddy onto Charles's. Then Gunnar jumped into the front seat and the chief swung up into the driver's seat next to him. He started the truck and pulled slowly out of the parking lot. Behind them came the three Littleton fire department trucks, filled with the rest of the firefighters, all in uniform. Lizzie turned around to wave to her dad, and he grinned and waved back. She gave Cody a big squeeze, and Cody gave her a happy snuffling kiss in return. Lizzie knew that this little puppy had found the perfect home.

PUPPY TIPS

A puppy is a big, big responsibility, for kids *and* for adults. Before people get a puppy or a dog, they should be sure they are ready. Puppies and dogs need lots of care and love — but even with the best care, they can be a real handful! Puppies make “mistakes” in the house. They chew things. They have lots and lots of energy! And grown dogs can be a handful, too. They might bark, or dig in the yard, or jump up on visitors. If you’re going to be a dog owner, you have to be prepared to deal with all of that — with a smile! It’s all worth it for the special kind of love our dogs give us in return.

Dear Reader,

I am very sorry to have to tell you that my dog Django, the sweetest, happiest black Lab ever, has died. He was eleven years old, which is pretty old in dog years. We had so many wonderful times together.

I will always treasure my memories of Django, starting from when I brought him home as a tiny puppy. It makes me smile just to think about how cute he was!

It's never easy to lose a pet that you have loved, but your memories will help to keep your pet alive in your heart.

Yours from the Puppy Place,
Ellen Miles

ABOUT THE AUTHOR

Ellen Miles is crazy about dogs, and loves to write about their different personalities. She is the author of more than 28 books, including the Puppy Place and Taylor-Made Tales series, as well as *The Pied Piper* and other Scholastic Classics. Ellen loves to be outdoors every day, walking, biking, skiing, or swimming, depending on the season. She also loves to read, cook, explore her beautiful state, and hang out with friends and family. She lives in Vermont.

If you love animals, be sure to read all the adorable stories in the Puppy Place series!